Goldilocks *and the* Three Bears

First Aladdin Paperbacks Edition September 1998

Aladdin Paperbacks
An imprint of Simon & Schuster Children's Publishing Division
1230 Avenue of the Americas
New York, NY 10020

READY-TO-READ is a registered trademark of Simon & Schuster, Inc.
Also available in a Simon & Schuster Books for Young Readers Edition.
The text for this book was set in Utopia.
Printed and bound in the United States of America
10 9 8 7 6 5 4 3 2 1

The Library of Congress has cataloged the Simon & Schuster
Books for Young Readers Edition as follows:
Miles, Betty
Goldilocks and the three bears / by Betty Miles ; illustrated by Bari Weissman.
p. cm. — (Ready-to-read)
Summary: Tells in simple dialogue the story of three bears who return home
from a walk to find a little girl asleep in Baby Bear's bed.
ISBN 0-689-81787-8 (hc)
[1. Folklore. 2. Bears Folklore.] I. Weissman, Bari, ill. II. Goldilocks and the
three bears. English. III. Title. IV. Series.
PZ8.1.M5995Go 1998
398.22—dc21
[E]   97-16008
CIP   AC
ISBN 0-689-81786-X (pbk)

Goldilocks *and the* Three Bears

Written by
Betty Miles

Illustrated by
Bari Weissman

Ready-to-Read

Aladdin Paperbacks

OLD STORIES FOR NEW READERS

Goldilocks and the Three Bears is an old story, and old stories are good for new readers. When they know what is going to happen, it's easier to read the words that tell about it.

Old stories often use the same words, like "Somebody was sitting in my chair!" over and over again. A new reader begins to expect those words, to enjoy them, and to learn them. The words in this story, like "too hot," "too cold," and "just right" are fun to say and easy to read.

You give your new reader a good start when you read out loud to each other. In this book, all the words are the characters' talk. Your child can read one character's words and you can read another's.

Take time to enjoy the story and the pictures. You can help your reader by talking about what is happening on the page and what might happen next. You can point to familiar words in the pictures. You can point to words that rhyme, and you can help by asking what sound a word begins with.

Most of all, you can help by reading together often. Your new reader can read with you or with a grandparent, a babysitter, an older brother, sister, or a friend. New readers love to share their books!

PART 1

Oh, look,
a little house!

Hello?
Hello?
Is anybody home?

Nobody home.
Look—three chairs
and three bowls!

This chair is too hard.

This chair
is too soft.

This chair is just right.

Oh!
Oh, no!
The chair broke!

Look—porridge!

OW!
This porridge is too hot.

Ooh,
this porridge is too cold.

Ahh.
This porridge is just right.
Mmm!

I'm sleepy.

Look—three beds!

This bed
is too hard.

This bed
is too soft.

This bed is just right.
Good night!
Zzzzzzzzzz.

PART 2

The 3 Bears

I want my porridge now!

Somebody was sitting
in my chair!

Somebody was sitting
in *my* chair!

Somebody was sitting
in *my* chair,
and it broke!

21

Somebody was eating
my porridge.

Somebody was eating
my porridge!

23

Somebody was
eating *my* porridge,
and now it's all gone!

Look!

Somebody was sleeping
in my bed!

Somebody was sleeping
in *my* bed!

Somebody was sleeping
in *my* bed—

27

AND THERE SHE IS NOW!

Oh!

Oh, no!

Oh!

Goodbye!

THE END